The First American Cookbook

A Facsimile of "American Cookery," 1796
by Amelia Simmons

W e all know the first rule of cooking:

wash your hands!

So let me come clean from the start:

this is a made-up tale.

For while there really was an Amelia Simmons,

who wrote America's first cookbook,

we don't know much about her.

Her cookbook tells us that she lived

during Revolutionary times,

and called herself "an American orphan."

But the details of her life are lost,

simmered away in the pot of time.

So why not start from scratch

and whip up something delicious about her?

For Vicki, who has passed her love of cooking to her daughters,
Keelia, Meghan, and Aili, and now to her grandsons,
Max and Eliot—D.H.

For Pia and Isabel—G.P.

INDEPENDENCE
CAKE

* A *

REVOLUTIONARY
CONFECTION

INSPIRED BY

Amelia Simmons

WHOSE TRUE HISTORY
IS UNFORTUNATELY
UNKNOWN

*

written by Deborah Hopkinson

illustrated by Giselle Potter

schwartz & wade books · new york

Let us imagine Amelia Simmons's father was a soldier,
lost in the war for independence.
Soon his poor widow would follow, succumbing to smallpox
and leaving our poor girl alone in the world.

The Leading Town Ladies asked, "What shall we do with Amelia?"
The answer was clear to all: "She must go to Mrs. Bean."
Amelia would become a "bound girl,"
taken in by a family to help with chores
so the town would be spared the cost of keeping her.

And Mrs. Bean needed help!
She had six strapping sons
but no daughter of her own.
(Definitely a recipe for domestic disaster in 1789.)

"Hello, Mrs. Bean?" Amelia called
into the kitchen when she arrived.
Then she spied a hand waving weakly
under stacks of shirts, piles of plates,
and mountains of mending.
"Don't despair, Mrs. Bean. I'm here!"

Amelia was as strong and young as the new nation itself.
From that day on,

she cleaned clothes,

scrubbed pots,

picked apples,

fed the chickens, and gathered the eggs.

She learned to spin

and knit

and sew,

quilt

and weave

and hoe.

Each evening, Amelia brought Mrs. Bean a cup of tea

and a thick slice of honey cake.

Mrs. Bean sighed with contentment,

resting her feet for what seemed like the first time in years.

"Thank you, my dear," she said.

"You've brightened our lives like a star on the flag."

"Amelia," said Mrs. Bean one day,
"you've always done everything I've asked,
and have even learned to read
by helping little Billy with his letters.
Is there any service I can do for you?"

Amelia had a ready answer.
"Well, all your cookbooks are
from England.
But we are independent now.
I want to learn
good, plain American cookery
and share recipes with my fellow citizens."

Chores—and cooking, too?
For Mrs. Bean, that was the icing on the cake!

Soon Amelia was up to her elbows in flour.

She learned to boil, broil, bake, and braise.

Tarts, creams, and custards?

She took charge like General Washington himself.

First, Amelia learned to cook the best English dishes.
She turned out rice puddings, bread puddings,
lemon, plum, and quince puddings.
She preserved peaches, pickled cucumbers,
and made marvelous marmalades.

Then, once she'd mastered the old favorites,

Amelia came up with new recipes using American ingredients.

There was winter squash pudding, perfect on an autumn day.

And she used cornmeal to make scrumptious flapjacks with maple syrup.

The Bean boys demolished stacks of them!

Just like her times, Amelia was revolutionary.

She invented a new way of baking using potash

to help her cakes rise.

And what delicious cakes they were!

Whenever she went to town,

Mrs. Bean bragged about Amelia,

boasting of her cakes and how the Bean boys loved them.

So it's no surprise that one fine morning,
a delegation of Leading Town Ladies arrived.
Amelia served tea biscuits with strawberry preserves.

For a long time there was only chewing and smiling.

Then the First Town Lady cleared her throat.
"As you know, our nation has just elected
General Washington our president."
"Long live George Washington!" everyone bellowed.
(Everybody, that is, except for the Bean boys, who had
sneaked in for biscuits and whose mouths were full.)

Washington!

"Our new president will soon be inaugurated in New York City," she went on.
"To mark this momentous occasion, people from all over
are sending gifts to be displayed in Federal Hall."

The First Town Lady stopped to lick her finger,
so the Second Town Lady put in,
"Amelia, we'd be proud if you would agree
to bake a cake in his honor."

Amelia clapped her hands.

"I know just the thing: an Independence Cake.

Though to feed all those guests, we'll need more than one."

Amelia got busy. She used (among other things):

twenty pounds of flour,

fifteen of sugar, and ten of butter;

four dozen eggs (beaten well, of course!);

a quart of brandy; spices, currants, and raisins;

and lots and lots of yeast

to be sure the cakes would rise

to this auspicious occasion.

Amelia's Independence Cakes
were baked to perfection.
Then, together with the boys,
she frosted them with sugar
and dressed them with gold leaf
till they shone like her hopes for the land she loved.

"How many do we have?"
our plucky patriot asked
when they were done.

CONNECTICUT

DELAWARE

MASSACHUSETTS

NEW HAMPSHIRE

NORTH CAROLINA

PENNSYLVANIA

"Thirteen," said little Billy Bean. "One for each colony."

"Let's name them together, boys," she said.

"In alphabetical order, if you please:

Connecticut, Delaware, Georgia, Maryland,

Massachusetts, New Hampshire, New Jersey, New York,

North Carolina, Pennsylvania, Rhode Island, South Carolina,

and of course, Virginia."

Mr. Bean hitched up the horses,
and everyone piled in with all the cakes.

Then off they went, unfurling flags and singing songs.
The Leading Town Ladies and the Leading Town Men
followed in a patriotic procession
all the way to Federal Hall.

There, Amelia Simmons,
soon-to-be authoress of *American Cookery*,
the first American cookbook,
presented a slice of Independence Cake
to George Washington,
the first American president.

He proclaimed it . . .

"Delicious!"

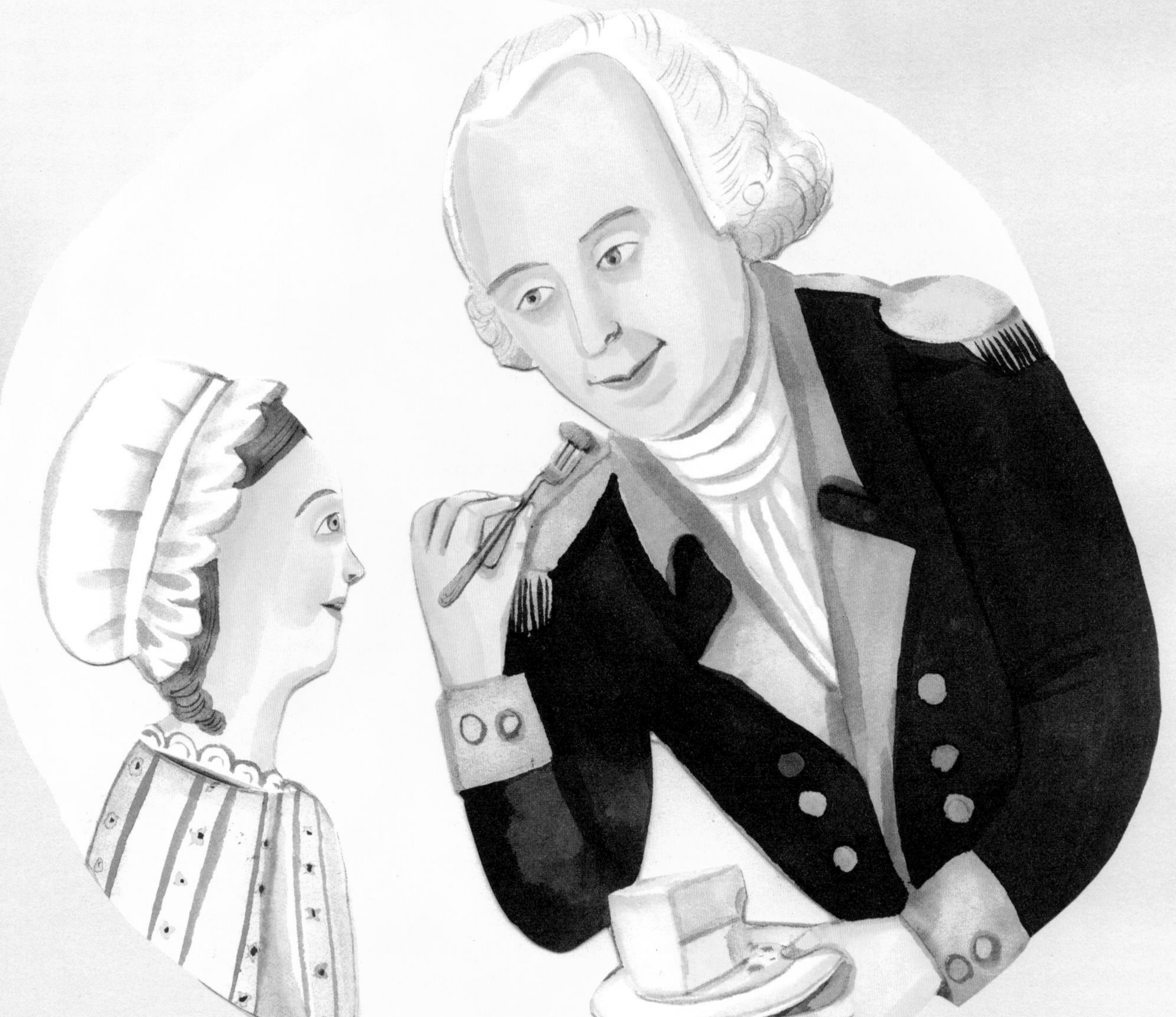

Amelia's Recipe for Independence Cake

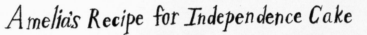

Twenty pound flour, 15 pound Sugar,
10 pound butter, 4 dozen eggs,
one quart wine, 1 quart brandy,
1 ounce nutmeg,
cinnamon, cloves, mace, of each 3 ounces,
two pound citron,
currants and raisins 5 pound each,
1 quart yeast;
when baked, frost with loaf Sugar;
dress with ... gold leaf.

AUTHOR'S NOTE

Amelia Simmons was indeed a real person, but just as the story says, little is known about her. We do know that her book, *American Cookery*, published in 1796, was the first cookbook written by an American. Since Amelia identifies herself as "an American orphan," historians believe she may have had to make her way in the world as a servant or cook.

Amelia's cookbook was based primarily on English culinary tradition. But it also featured new dishes that make use of ingredients more common in America, such as cornmeal. In addition, her cookbook was the first to recommend using "potash," sometimes called "pearl ash," which is similar to the baking powder we use today. Amelia also introduced new words, such as "cookies," based on the word "koejke," borrowed from Dutch settlers in America.

The second edition of Amelia's cookbook, also published in 1796, contains the first known recipe for Independence Cake. It is similar to recipes for Election Day cakes, which were baked for festive occasions or town meetings in both England and in America. Certainly, in the early days of America, Election Day was a time to come together to celebrate our democracy. And what better way to celebrate than to eat some delicious cake? George Washington was inaugurated the nation's first president at Federal Hall in New York City on April 30, 1789. There is no record that he ate Independence Cake on that day.

Text copyright © 2017 by Deborah Hopkinson
Jacket art and interior illustrations copyright © 2017 by Giselle Potter

All rights reserved. Published in the United States by Schwartz & Wade Books,
an imprint of Random House Children's Books, a division of Penguin Random House LLC, New York.

Schwartz & Wade Books and the colophon are trademarks of Penguin Random House LLC.
Visit us on the Web! randomhousekids.com
Educators and librarians, for a variety of teaching tools, visit us at RHTeachersLibrarians.com

Library of Congress Cataloging-in-Publication Data
Hopkinson, Deborah, author.
Independence Cake : a revolutionary confection inspired by Amelia Simmons,
whose true history is unfortunately unknown
Deborah Hopkinson and Giselle Potter. — First edition.
pages cm
Includes a list of ingredients, and links to various recipes for Independence Cake.
Summary: In this fictional story, Amelia Simmons, writer of the first American cookbook, creates an
Independence Cake in 1789 to offer the newly elected President, George Washington.
ISBN 978-0-385-39017-0 (alk. paper) — ISBN 978-0-385-39018-7 (glb : alk. paper)
ISBN 978-0-385-39019-4 (ebook)
1. Simmons, Amelia—Juvenile fiction. 2. Cooks—United States—Juvenile fiction. 3. Cake—Juvenile
fiction. 4. United States—History—1783–1815—Juvenile fiction. [1. Simmons, Amelia—Fiction.
2. Cooks—Fiction. 3. Cake—Fiction. 4. United States—History—1783-1815—Fiction.]
I. Potter, Giselle, illustrator. II. Title.
PZ7.H778125 In 2017
[E]—dc23
2014040302

The text of this book is set in Fournier.
The illustrations were rendered in watercolor and ink.
Book design by Rachael Cole

MANUFACTURED IN CHINA
2 4 6 8 10 9 7 5 3 1
First Edition

Learn more about Election Cakes, Amelia Simmons, and modern versions of Election Day cake recipes online

csmonitor.com/The-Culture/Food/Stir-It-Up/2012/1105/Election-Cake-An-American-tradition

londoneats.wordpress.com/tag/amelia-simmons/

newenglandrecipes.org/html/election-cake.html

whatscookingamerica.net/History/Cakes/ElectionCake.html

To read a copy of *American Cookery:*

  books.google.com/books?id=_6CggcPs3iQC&printsec=

  frontcover&source=gbs_ge_summary_r&cad=0#v=onepage&q&f=false